Fabulous Five-Minute Stories

The Pitiful Pirates

Written by Jane Arlington

Illustrated by Meredith Johnson

Reader's Digest Young Families

"Five minutes until lunchtime, Lydia dear!" called Lydia's mother.

"Okay, Mom!" Lydia called back. She was enjoying the beautiful day. Seagulls cawed overhead. The warm water lapped gently against the side of her raft. Lydia dipped her fingers in the water and lay back. Her eyelids drooped.

A seagull screeched, and Lydia stood up. "Has it been five minutes already?" she wondered, rubbing her eyes. She looked toward the beach. She rubbed her eyes harder. The shoreline had vanished. All around her was open blue water.

Where was the beach? The sun was directly overhead. Lydia didn't even know which way to row.

Trying not to panic, she shaded her eyes and peered carefully in every direction. There was nothing but a hazy line where the sea met the sky.

But wait! What was that? Lydia thought she spotted something on the horizon.

It was a sail. Lydia paddled in that direction as fast as she could. Luckily the wind sprang up, and she was soon close enough to see the ship clearly.

"Hmm," she said to herself, pausing on her oars a moment to catch her breath. "I am sure I have seen that kind of sail before. But where?"

With a sudden shock, she realized that the sail showed
the Jolly Roger, the symbol of pirates everywhere. Too late!
She felt rough hands grab her arms. Up, up, up she went,
until she was hauled aboard.

Lydia was pushed roughly onto the deck.

"Fie, 'tis but a puny stripling!" growled a tall and important-looking man. Obviously, he was the captain. "Check her pockets for treasure!" he ordered.

"I'm wearing a bathing suit," Lydia pointed out. "Just where would I carry treasure?"

"She's a cheeky one, forsooth," growled a pirate with an eye patch. "If there be no treasure, make the wretch walk the plank!"

"The plank! The plank!" came a chorus of voices.

Things were definitely not getting off to the right start.

"Now let's not be hasty," said Lydia, as she eyed the pirates carrying a long plank of wood across the deck. "See, I'm just a kid on vacation with my parents. I got blown off course and . . ."

"Enough babble from you, you little pipsqueak!" said the captain.

Suddenly the wind whirled around them. The creaky ship began to rise up and down with the swelling waves.

In an instant, the pirates dropped the plank and ran. One staggered toward the hold, racing to get below. The others clutched the railings, moaning.

"Whatever is the matter with all of you?" asked Lydia, whose curiosity had overcome her fear. "Anyone would think you were seasick!"

The captain nodded weakly. "Aye, that we be," he said. "We don't like rough waves. And we never seem to find any treasure. Truth be told, we are not very good pirates."

"Well, perhaps it's time to change careers," said Lydia. "What other things do you like to do?"

The captain looked left and right, then spoke in a low voice. "We like to cook," he admitted. "And we're pretty good at it. In fact, all the other pirate ships come around whenever we drop anchor and ask us to cook for them."

"Well, then, why don't you think about going into the restaurant business?" suggested Lydia.

"What a strange notion," he murmured, and he began pacing the deck thoughtfully. The wind died down, and the other pirates gathered around him. "By gum, we'll do it! We'll give up pirating and open a restaurant!"

"To thank you for your idea," the captain said to Lydia, "we will take you wherever you wish to go."

The pirate ship turned in the direction that Lydia had come from. Before long, land came into view. Gently, the pirates lowered Lydia down to her raft.

"Bye!" she waved to the pirates. "Good luck with your new careers!"

The ship turned away, and Lydia rowed toward the beach. As the wind was now blowing against her, she soon needed a rest. She leaned over her oars, and her eyes began to close.

The caw of a seagull startled her awake. Lydia was back
at the beach! Her parents were right where she had last seen
them. But now they were standing, waiting for her.

"Ready for lunch, sweetie?" her mother called.

Was it really just lunchtime? Lydia looked up. The sun
was still directly overhead. Had it all been a dream?

"There's a wonderful new seafood restaurant we want to try," her mother was saying, as they walked down the beach. A moment later, they rounded the bend and saw it . . .

Maybe it hadn't been a dream.